EXPLORE THE WORLD

SOCIAL SCIENCE

SO-DZE-989

The Firefighter

MICHÈLE DUFRESNE

N.Y. F.D.

PIONEER VALLEY EDUCATIONAL PRESS, INC

I am a firefighter.

Here is my helmet.
I can put on my helmet.

helmet

jacket

gloves

pants

boots

5

Here is the fire truck.
We go to the fire
in the fire truck.

MORE TO EXPLORE

There are three
kinds of fire trucks.

PUMPER TRUCKS

LADDER TRUCKS

TANKER TRUCKS

Here is my dog.
My dog is going
to the fire, too.

Here is a ladder.
I can climb the ladder.

Look! Here is the fire.

Here is the hose.
We can put the fire out!